I, *Geronimo Stilton*, have a lot of mouse friends, but none as **spooky** as my friend CREEPELLA VON CACKLEFUR! She is an enchanting and MYSTERIOUS mouse with a pet bat named **Bitewing**. Creepella lives in a CEMETERY, sleeps in a marble **sarcophagus**, and drives a **hearse**. By night she is a special effects and set designer for SCARY FILMS, and by day she's studying to become a journalist! Her father, Boris von Cacklefur, runs the funeral home Fabumouse Funerals, and the von Cacklefur family owns the CREEPY Cacklefur Castle, which sits on top of a skull-shaped mountain in MYSTERIOUS VALLEY.

YIKES! I'm a real 'fraidy mouse, but even I think Creepella and her family are AWFULLY fascinating. I can't wait for you to read this fa-mouse-ly funny and SPECTACULARLY SPOOKY tale!

Geronimo Stilton

Creepella von Cacklefur

Bitewing

Billy Squeakspeare

Grandpa Frankenstein

An extremely mad scientist and an expert in Egyptian mummies.

A journalist who lives in Mysterious Valley and solves spooky cases with her inseparable pet bat, Bitewing.

A famous writer and friend of Creepella.

Shivereen

Grandma Crypt

Snip and Snap

Creepella's favorite niece.

Troublemaking twins and expert spies.

Dolores

Kafka

She loves spiders, and her pet is a gigantic tarantula named Dolores.

The von Cacklefur family's pet cockroach.

Booey the Poltergeist

The mischievous ghost who haunts Cacklefur Castle.

Boneham

The butler to the von Cacklefur family, and a snob right down to the tips of his whiskers.

Baby

He was adopted and raised with love by the von Cacklefurs.

Madame LaTomb

The family housekeeper. A ferocious were-canary nests in her hair.

Chef Stewrat

The cook at Cacklefur Castle. He dreams of creating the ultimate stew.

Boris von Cacklefur

Creepella's father, and the funeral director at Fabumouse Funerals.

Chompers

The von Cacklefur family's meat-eating guard plant.

Geronimo Stilton

CREEPELLA VON CACKLEFUR

THE HAUNTED DINOSAUR

Scholastic Inc.

Copyright © 2012 by Edizioni Piemme S.p.A., Palazzo Mondadori, Via Mondadori 1, 20090 Segrate, Italy. International Rights © Atlantyca S.p.A. English translation © 2017 by Atlantyca S.p.A.

The publisher does not have any control over and does not assume any responsibility for author or third-party websites or their content.

GERONIMO STILTON names, characters, and related indicia are copyright, trademark, and exclusive license of Atlantyca S.p.A. All rights reserved. The moral right of the author has been asserted. Based on an original idea by Elisabetta Dami. www.geronimostilton.com

Published by Scholastic Inc., *Publishers since 1920*, 557 Broadway, New York, NY 10012. SCHOLASTIC and associated logos are trademarks and/or registered trademarks of Scholastic Inc.

Stilton is the name of a famous English cheese. It is a registered trademark of the Stilton Cheese Makers' Association. For more information, go to www.stiltoncheese.com.

ISBN 978-1-338-08789-5

Text by Geronimo Stilton
Original title *Il risveglio del brividosauro*
Cover by Giuseppe Ferrario (pencils and inks) and Giulia Zaffaroni (color)
Illustrations by Ivan Bigarella (pencils), Antonio Campo (ink), and Daria Cerchi (color)
Graphics by Yuko Egusa

Special thanks to AnnMarie Anderson
Translated by Lidia Morson Tramontozzi
Interior design by Becky James

10 9 8 7 6 5 4 3 2 1   17 18 19 20 21

Printed in the U.S.A.   40

First printing, 2017

My Whiskers Still Tremble with Fright

If spooky stories give you **NIGHTMARES**; if you hide under the covers during **THUNDERSTORMS**; or if you're scared of the dark, monsters, or ghosts, then you'd better close this book **RIGHT NOW**!

Oops . . . so sorry! I haven't introduced myself yet. My name is Stilton, *Geronimo Stilton*, and I run *The Rodent's Gazette*, the most famouse newspaper on Mouse Island.

Do you want to know what I'm squeaking about?

The book you're holding contains a story written by the one and only CREEPELLA VON

CACKLEFUR. She's the spookiest mouse I know! She lives in Mysterious Valley, where the strangest adventures seem to take place. In fact, this story is so **spooktacular**, it will make your fur, ears, and tail quiver with fright!

Yikes!

Now that you've been warned, do you still want to read this **SCARY** tale? Are you sure? Absolutely, pawsitively, double-dog-daringly sure? Well, all right then! I may as well start from the beginning . . .

It was a warm evening in early spring. The setting sun cast a shadow over the roofs of New Mouse City. I was sitting in my favorite pawchair in my cozy living room, sipping a cup of hot melted cheddar.

My nephew Benjamin was sitting on the

floor, engrossed in one of the  BOOKS from my library. His class was planning a trip to **Fossil Forest** that week, so he was reading all about it.

"Look, Uncle!" he squeaked excitedly. "This piece of cheese FOSSIL goes back thousands of years."

He showed me an illustration in the book he was reading, Traveling Through the Jurassic Era. I was about to take a look when there was a LOUD knock at the door.

KNOCK! KNOCK! KNOCK!

"Who could that be?" I wondered aloud. But when I opened the door, there was no one there! I looked down and saw a flat stone tied up with a purple bow. I looked around to see who had left it, but the street was deserted. HOW STRANGE!

"Who was it, Uncle G?" Benjamin asked.

I said I wasn't sure. Then I showed him the **stone** tied with the bow. We quickly realized it wasn't **ONE** stone, but **TWO**! The tablets were tied together, and there were sheets of paper between them.

"This is really unusual," I murmured as I untied the bow . . .

"**ACK!**" I squeaked.

A fossil of an enormouse **COCKROACH** sat on top of the papers. Beside it was a *handwritten* note on a piece of coffin-shaped paper. I immediately recognized Creepella von Cacklefur's scented purple ink!

I read the note aloud:

Geronimo, do you remember our last adventure? I wrote it down so you can publish it. Here you go!

A chill ran down my fur.

"Of course I remember!" I squeaked. "My whiskers still **tremble** with fright whenever I think about it."

"What **ADVENTURE** is she talking about, Uncle?" Benjamin asked, his eyes glowing with excitement. "Will you read it to me, please?"

"It's a little **SCARY**, but I'll read it if you're sure . . ." I warned him.

"I'm sure!" he squeaked eagerly.

So I made myself **comfortable** and began to read . . .

THE HAUNTED DINOSAUR

STORY AND ILLUSTRATIONS BY CREEPELLA VON CACKLEFUR

A Surprise for Geronimo

It was a FOGGY morning in Gloomeria. A pale ray of SUNSHINE flickered feebly through the clouds, barely illuminating the front door of Squeakspeare Mansion. A GLOOMY silence filled the ancient mansion. The thirteen ghosts who lived there had spent the entire night cleaning the place from TOP to BOTTOM.

Now they were exhausted, and they had all fallen into a deep sleep.

The desk in the mansion's study was overflowing with piles of books, stacks and stacks of PAPER, and notebooks and memo pads filled with scribbled notes. Someone was busy RESEARCHING and writing the interminable, inexhaustible, endless ENCYCLOPEDIA OF GHOSTS. But at that particular moment, that someone was not at his desk. Instead, he was a passenger in the **Turborapid 3000**, Creepella von Cacklefur's CREEPY convertible.

Who is Creepella von Cacklefur? She's the **eeriest** journalist in Mysterious Valley!

"W-where are we going?" the mouse in the

backseat stuttered. "I should be working . . ."

It was the newspaper mouse *Geronimo Stilton*! He was sitting in the backseat next to Creepella's niece **Shivereen**, and the von Cacklefur family's pet cockroach, **KAFKA**.

Creepella's pet bat flew in circles around Geronimo's head. Grandfather Frankenstein rode in the passenger seat, a 🅂🄼🄰🄻🄻 package in his lap.

"Oh, hush, Geronimo!" Creepella replied

We're almost there!

as she sped through the countryside. "You don't want to miss it, do you?"

"M-miss what?" Geronimo asked nervously. He would rather be holed up in Squeakspeare Mansion, happily working on the ENCYCLOPEDIA OF GHOSTS.

"Why, the opening of the exhibition, of course!" Creepella replied. She honked her horn in greeting as she zoomed past her father's HEARSE. The family's butler,

Yes, Auntie!

Is everyone here?

Boneham, wasn't far behind. He was traveling by **motorcycle**, with Grandma Crypt in his sidecar.

"Your entire family seems to be attending this event," Geronimo observed. "But I still don't know what **exhibition** you're squeaking about!"

Creepella smiled as the wind **ruffled** her raven-black hair.

"Of course we're all attending!" she replied breezily. "We wouldn't miss it for the **gloomiest** funeral in the world. Isn't that right, Shivereen?"

"Yes!" replied Shivereen. "I wouldn't skip it for the biggest **HORROR FILM** marathon!"

Kafka **wiggled** his antennas in agreement.

"I wouldn't miss it for the **Great Ball of the Mummies**!" piped up Grandpa Frankenstein.

"But what's this exhibition about?" Geronimo asked again, exasperated.

Creepella brought her Turborapid 3000 to an **ABRUPT** stop in front of the Gloomeria Science Museum.

"You'll find out soon enough!"

An Exhibition Worth Waiting For

A large CROWD had gathered in front of the science museum. Everyone was waiting impatiently for the doors to open while the mayor, Charles Chatterpaws, gave a long-winded speech. Rodents everywhere were yawning and fidgeting, their whiskers drooping with boredom.

"Dear citizens of Gloomeria," the mayor droned, "today we celebrate this auspicious event. We have been waiting for many gloomy months for the opening day of this great exhibition . . ."

The mayor's wife, Carol, took a step closer.

"**Cut it, darling!**" she whispered in her husband's ear.

"Huh?" the mayor replied. "What did you say?"

Carol squeaked a bit louder.

"**Cut it, dear!**" she repeated.

"I'm not quite finished yet," the mayor protested. "Just a few more —"

"**THE RIBBON!**" Carol squeaked, exasperated.

The mayor took one look at his wife and **SHUT** his mouth. Then he sliced through the purple ribbon in front of him with an **OVERSIZED** pair of scissors.

SNIP!

Everyone quickly **RUSHED** into the museum, eager to see the exhibit. Geronimo looked up and saw this banner hanging over the museum entrance:

WELCOME TO THE EXHIBITION OF THE YEAR: THE HAUNTED DINOSAURS OF MYSTERIOUS VALLEY!

Geronimo gulped. His whiskers quivered with fright. He was a huge scaredy-mouse! Then he noticed two **strange-looking** rodents in a corner.

"Who are they?" he asked Creepella, intrigued.

"Those are the most famouse ARCHAEOLOGISTS in Gloomeria: Ignazio Dustysnout and Petra Fossilfur!" his friend explained. "After years and years of research and archaeological excavations, they've finally finished reconstructing the skeletons of the dinosaurs that lived in Mysterious Valley

millions of years ago!"

"I've been looking forward to this for decades. This will be the perfect opportunity for me to test my latest INVENTION!" Grandpa Frankenstein said.

Grandpa Frankenstein was a professor and an inventor. In his paws he held a small black box with **two buttons**: One was RED, and the other was GREEN.

"It's a **borebuster remote!**" he explained gleefully. "If someone is boring me, I point the remote control at him, press the RED button, and . . . BOOM! He's instantly **immobilized**!"

"Moldy mozzarella!" Geronimo gasped. "That is pure evil! Will he stay frozen forever?!"

"Of course not!" Grandpa Frankenstein

replied. "He'll be stunned for a couple of seconds . . . er, I mean, at the most, it will be a few minutes. He won't be able to squeak or move a paw!"

Creepella hugged her grandfather.

"Grandfather, you're a genius!"

she squeaked proudly. "May i try it?"

Grandpa Frankenstein handed her the remote.

"Press the red button, but only the RED button!" he told her. "Understand?"

"Yup!" she squeaked. Then Creepella pointed the remote directly at Geronimo.

"Creepella, please don't . . ." he protested.

But it was **TOO LATE**! She had already pressed the button. A red light illuminated Geronimo's face and he was immobilized immediately.

"Auntie!" Shivereen exclaimed. "Now how are you going to move him around?"

Tee, hee!

Don't do it!

"That won't be a **problem**," Creepella chuckled. "He'll be back to normal soon enough, right Grandpa?"

"Of course I'm back to normal!" Geronimo squeaked as he wiggled his paws. "Please don't **freeze** me again!"

"Drat!" Creepella muttered. "That didn't last long. How did it feel, Geronimo?"

But before he could answer, she turned toward her grandfather.

"What's the **GREEN** button for?" she asked, curious. "Can I **press** it?"

Grandpa Frankenstein quickly **SNATCHED** the remote from her.

"That part of my invention still needs a little tweaking," he mumbled. "But enough of that! Let's go see the **exhibition**!"

A DINOSAUR FOR EVERYONE

It was the most incredible exhibition anyone had ever seen. The crowd gathered around each exhibit, gaping at the rarest dinosaur skeletons in Mysterious Valley. The von Cacklefur family was particularly excited. Even Geronimo had to admit he had NEVER been to such a remarkable event.

The exhibition included dinosaurs of all shapes and SIZES.

Grandma Crypt liked the smallest dino the best. "What an adorably SPINE-TINGLING little minisaurus!" she squeaked with delight.

Snip and Snap preferred the very odd **bizarrosaurus**.

"He looks so strange!" they said, giggling.

"My favorite is the **gulposaurus**!" declared Chef Stewrat. "I'm positive he would have liked my stew!"

Shivereen nodded and pointed to another.

"I like the **sillysaurus**," she said. "Did you see his little laughing face? Then again, the **snorosaurus** is also adorable. And the **megasaurus** is really **impressive**!"

Grandpa Frankenstein seemed to be the only one not having a good time. He hadn't even used his **borebuster remote**!

Everyone at the exhibition was so **excited** to be there; no one was being **boring** at all!

Grandpa Frankenstein looked around sadly.

23

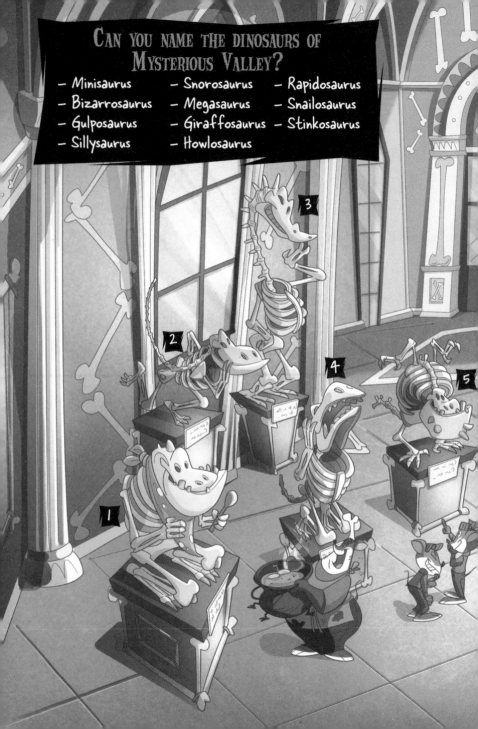

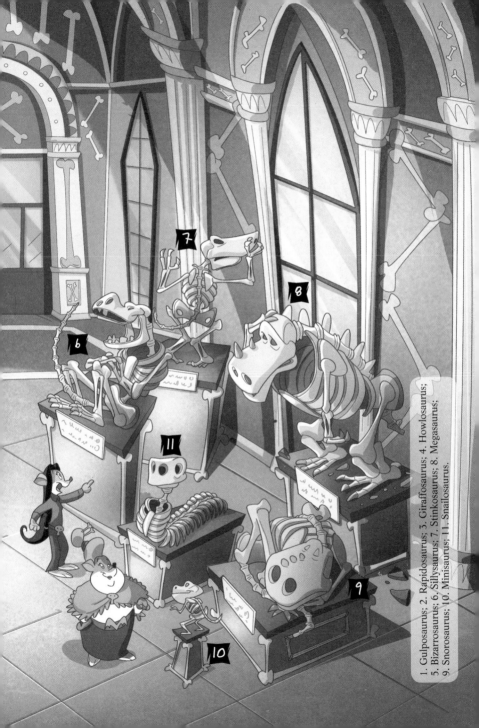

1. Gulposaurus; 2. Rapidosaurus; 3. Giraffosaurus; 4. Howlosaurus; 5. Bizarrosaurus; 6. Sillysaurus; 7. Stinkosaurus; 8. Megasaurus; 9. Snorosaurus; 10. Minisaurus; 11. Snailosaurus.

"Maybe I'll try it randomly on someone!" he said.

"You can't stun a rodent without a reason!" Grandma Crypt SCOLDED him.

"I'd argue that you shouldn't stun a rodent even if you DO have a reason!" Geronimo squeaked under his breath.

"You're right," Grandpa Frankenstein sighed. "I'll only try it if I come across a rodent more suffocating than a casket buried in a bog."

Let's see . . .

While the pros and cons of using the remote were being discussed, Geronimo began reading up on the exhibition.

"The next room is dedicated entirely to the exhibition's MAIN attraction," he told the von Cacklefurs.

"The **SPOOKOSAURUS** is supposed to be the SCARIEST, *creepiest*, most DREADFUL dinosaur that ever existed!"

Creepella hurried toward the door.

"Well, what are we waiting for?" she said eagerly. "Let's go check it out RIGHT NOW!"

On the way into the next room, Creepella's father, Boris von Cacklefur, caught Geronimo's ear. He was just DYING to tell some of his favorite scary jokes!

"Psst, Geronimo!" Boris squeaked. "Have you heard the one about the dinosaur?"

BORIS VON CACKLEFUR'S DINO JOKES

HEE HEE HEE

What's a dinosaur's favorite school subject?
Prehistory

Knock, knock.
Who's there?
Interrupting dinosaur.
Interrupting dino —
ROAAAAAR!

What time is it when a dinosaur sits on the hood of your car?
Time to get a new car!

What do you call a fossil that never wants to do any work?
Lazy bones!

HA HA HA HA

What's louder than two dinosaurs?
Three dinosaurs!

What do you call a dinosaur who is never late?
A promptosaurus!

Why did the dinosaur cross the road?
To eat the chicken on the other side!

HEE HEE HEE HEE

ONE SCARY DINOSAUR!

A large sign stood at the entrance to the hall that contained the spookosaurus skeleton. It rested on a stand made of small bones that had been tied together. Geronimo stopped to read it before he entered.

HERE LIES SPOOKOSAURUS! Do not enter if you get nauseous or are frightened easily.

"M-maybe I'll s-skip this room," he stammered after he read the sign.

"Oh no you don't,

Geronimo," Creepella said as she **grabbed** his paw and pushed him into the room.

Unfortunately, this caused Geronimo to trip over the sign. He knocked it down, and the bones SHATTERED into a thousand pieces.

"Geronimo!" Creepella squeaked, **exasperated**. "Look what you've done!"

"Me?" Geronimo replied. "You're the one who pushed me!"

Creepella peeked inside the room and gasped.

"Howling mummies!" she squeaked. "This dinosaur is **petrifying**!"

"Rats and bats!" Shivereen exclaimed, clapping her little paws in approval. "It's totally BLOODCURDLING!"

"Moldy mummy soup!" said Snip and Snap. "It's **HORRIFIC**!"

The terrifying spookosaurus skeleton **TOWERED** over all of them.

"Holey cheese!" Geronimo exclaimed as he tried not to faint with fear. A shiver ran down his spine. "Next to that fossil, the other d-dinosaurs look like little *worms*

on a piece of ch-cheese!"

The spookosaurus skeleton was so **BIG** it took up the entire room. And it was so **TALL** that the roof had been cut open to make room for the top of the skeleton's head! The spookosaurus's gigantic paws ended in long, sharp claws. Its mouth gaped open in a smirk that exposed its **RAZOR-SHARP** teeth. And its eyes were two massive, hollow holes that were as **DARK** as a bottomless well.

"Its smallest tooth is bigger than my largest pot!" Chef Stewrat observed.

Grandpa Frankenstein even forgot about his **remote control**. For a minute, he was the one who seemed stunned as he

peered up at the ancient monster in **admiration**.

In his **EXCITEMENT**, Grandpa didn't notice that his infamous rival,

SHAMLEY RATTENBAUM,

was standing right next to the spookosaurus! Shamley was wearing his usual old **PATCHED** jacket with a gardenia tucked in the buttonhole.

As soon as Shamley spotted Grandpa Frankenstein, he approached him with his usual **contempt**.

"I didn't think I'd meet so many **uncultured** rodents at such a prestigious museum," he said with a sniff of disdain.

The scientist clenched the borebuster remote in his paw.

"Watch your tongue, *Rotten*baum,"

Grandpa Frankenstein squeaked. "You don't want me to try my latest **device** on you!"

Shamley Rattenbaum laughed.

"I'm not afraid of you, **Dr. Frankenstinky!**" he teased Grandpa. "Anyway, I just noticed a certain similarity between you and this dinosaur . . ."

"Is it our backbones?" Grandpa replied. "Because at least I have one! You, on the other paw . . ."

Rattenbaum became as WHITE as a ghost, then as **red** as an overripe tomato.

"How dare you!" he replied as he plucked the gardenia from his buttonhole. He was about to throw it at his rival's snout, but Grandpa Frankenstein was quicker. He pointed the borebuster remote at Shamley and pressed the **RED** button.

Rattenbaum froze instantly.

He was as immobile as a mummified lizard! His eyes were the only part of his body that moved, and they darted back and forth, shooting DAGGERS at the entire von Cacklefur clan.

"Now he's the one that looks like a DINOSAUR!" joked Grandpa.

"I agree!" Boris chuckled.

"Looks like your new invention is a big SUCCESS!" Grandma Crypt observed.

"Yes, it works like a charm!" Shivereen said.

Creepella put up a paw to get everyone's attention.

"Shhhh," she said. "QUIET! It looks like the effects of the borebuster remote are wearing off. SHAMLEY IS MOVING!"

He looks so silly!

Ha, ha, ha!

Hee, hee, hee!

SHAMLEY IMMOBILIZED!

A Terrifying Surprise

Rattenbaum rolled his eyes, wrinkled his nose, and **STRETCHED** out his right paw and then his left paw. Grandpa Frankenstein was still celebrating his success, and he didn't notice Shamley charging toward him.

"Grandpa, **WATCH OUT**!" Creepella squeaked. But she was **TOO LATE**.

Shamley had **SNATCHED** the borebuster remote right out of Grandpa Frankenstein's paws! He held it above his

SHAMLEY IS MOVING!

head triumphantly.

"Aha!" Rattenbaum squeaked gleefully. "You'll be sorry you froze me, Professor!"

"Be careful, Rattenbaum." Geronimo warned him. "That device is not a TOY! Someone could get hurt."

"Is it proper to freeze a rodent for no reason?!" Shamley asked.

"Well, no it isn't. I do agree with you." Geronimo stuttered. "Still, it isn't safe —"

"Enough!" shouted Shamley. He turned and POINTED the remote control at Grandpa Frankenstein. The professor quickly ducked behind the spookosaurus's MASSIVE paw.

"It's payback time!" Rattenbaum said as he pressed the GREEN button with all his might.

"NO!" cried Grandpa Frankenstein as he flung himself at his rival. "NOT THE

GREEN BUTTON!"
TOO LATE!

Rattenbaum had already pressed the WR🌀NG button. A **BRIGHT-GREEN** ray shot out of the remote, hitting the giant spookosaurus skeleton in the snout. The fossil's fearsome face LIT UP with a menacing glow.

Grandpa Frankenstein's snout went as PALE as a slice of mozzarella.

"What have you done?" he moaned. "I have no idea what's going to happen now."

"Professor," Geronimo asked, a worried look on his snout. "You REALLY don't know what the green button does? Didn't you **invent** the remote yourself?"

"Scampering skeletons!" Creepella squeaked suddenly, her eyes wide. "I think I just figured out what the green button does . . ."

"The red button freezes things," Creepella whispered. "But the GREEN button brings things to life — even the thousand-year-old skeleton of a fossilized dinosaur! LOOK!"

Suddenly, the spookosaurus took a flying LEAP up to the roof of the building!

Chattering cheddar!

He's running away!

Oh no!

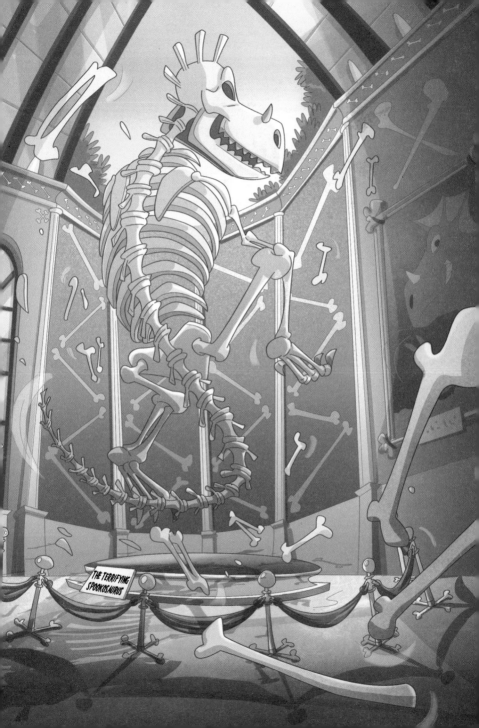

THE TERRIFYING
SPOOKOSAURUS

IT'S RAINING BONES!

The room became as quiet as a **TOMB**. Grandpa Frankenstein **pointed** an angry paw at Shamley Rattenbaum.

"Look what you've done!" Grandpa said accusingly.

"It's all your fault, **Frankenslime**," Rattenbaum replied haughtily. "After all, **YOUR** invention made the spookosaurus come to *life*! Who would invent something so horrible? And if you hadn't frozen me first —"

Creepella stepped between them.

"That's enough **fighting**!" she squeaked.

"Both of you! We have to figure out how to **ST◎P** that prehistoric monster before it **DESTROYS** Gloomeria!"

Grandpa nodded and headed for the exit.

"I'll head straight to my laboratory," he said. "Hopefully I can invent something to **FIX** this mess!"

An **infuriated** Shamley Rattenbaum stormed off in the opposite direction.

"Well, I'm going home to some **peace** and **QUIET**!" he shouted. "I've had enough!"

Meanwhile, the spookosaurus was on a **demolition** course out in front of the museum. The destructive dino was running over everything that crossed its path! Soon the lovely **garden** in front of the museum was

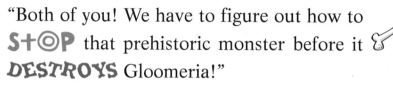

a mass of trampled white flowers. As the spookosaurus stomped down the street, it CRUSHED a row of cars, flattening them like cheddar pancakes!

Every so often, a few small bones would come loose from the spookosaurus's colossal skeleton. The bones rained down on the snouts of the rodents below.

"Heeeelp!" the fleeing rodents cried. "It's raining bones!"

The mayor pleaded for **calm** despite the chaos.

"Everything is under control!" he squeaked over the shouts of the rodents around him.

His wife tapped him on the back.

Run for your life!

"Darling, your car," she whispered.

He turned to his wife.

"What did you say, dear?" Mayor Chatterpaws asked.

"Look at your **CAR**," Carol repeated.

"What do you mean?" the mayor asked, confused.

"The spookosaurus just squashed your Jalopy 2000," Carol replied calmly, pointing to her husband's most prized possession.

"What?! Noooooo!" he sobbed, tears rolling down

his snout. "My baby! I **loved** that car so much!"

Geronimo, Creepella, and the rest of the von Cacklefurs scurried out of the museum just in time to see the mayor burst into tears.

"What an awful **MESS**!" Creepella exclaimed as she took in the disaster the spookosaurus had left in its wake.

"**We have to stop it!**" the mayor cried desperately.

Creepella nodded.

"Agreed," she said solemnly. "But how?"

The spookosaurus was busy plodding through the middle of town, **crushing** everything in its path. But suddenly, the skeleton stopped and raised its head as if something had hit it. Then it took off toward the edge of town at **top speed**.

"**Where's it g-going?**" Geronimo

stammered, his whiskers shaking with fright.

"That's the way to Rattenbaum Mansion!" Creepella gasped. "Let's follow it!"

The mayor threw his arms up. "I'm going back to CITY HALL," he squeaked. "Call me if there's any news!"

Let's go!

A CUP OF MOLDY TEA

Back at the Rattenbaum Mansion, Shamley's triplet granddaughters, Tilly, Milly, and Lilly, were lounging contentedly under the patched, wobbly gazebo in the mansion's overgrown gardens. A teapot, some chipped teacups, and a tray of moldy pastries sat on the table before them. The family's pet millipede, Ziggy, spotted the treats and began to DROOL in anticipation.

Unfortunately for Ziggy, the horrid moldy goodies weren't

for him, but for the sisters' prestigious guests: the triplets Lenny, **Benny**, and Denny Vandervermer.

The three young ratlets were descendants of one of the oldest families in Mysterious Valley. Their family boasted counts, dukes, viscounts, and marquises all over the genealogical tree. The Vendervermers prided themselves on their royal blood, yet everyone in the family seemed to be completely broke!

"How honored we are to visit . . ." Lenny began gallantly.

". . . after so many years . . ." continued Benny.

". . . of being away from the city!" Denny concluded.

"Oh no, the good fortune is all ours!" Milly replied.

"Would you like a **CUP** of moldy tea?" asked Lilly.

"Or an aged PASTRY?" suggested Tilly.

At the word *pastry*, Ziggy began to whimper hungrily. But no one was paying any attention to him. The triplets were more interested in entertaining their dashing young guests.

Ziggy's duty for the day was playing DJ. He was in charge of changing the records on the ancient gramophone, and he was doing a fabumouse job. His favorite record was playing. It was Tear in the Tempest by Lyrica Sonnetail, and the notes of the song "Morbid Whining" hung in the air.

The three noblerats were impressed with the millipede's musical taste.

"What an absolutely eerie record!" Lenny said admiringly.

"IT'S SO GHASTLY AND GOULISH!" Benny agreed.

"YES, it's DEEPLY DEPRESSING!" Denny concluded.

Ziggy noticed that the triplets were distracted by the noblerats, and the noblerats were distracted by the music. So he quickly snatched a rotten grasshopper pastry during the second verse of "Mournful Lament."

"YUM!" he whispered as he gulped it down in one bite. Ziggy was about to grab another treat when he noticed Shamley Rattenbaum scurrying along the path to the mansion. Shamley seemed disoriented. He was mumbling to himself as he stormed toward the gazebo in the garden.

"Isn't that your grandfather?" Lenny asked.

"He looks really UPSET," continued Benny.

"Maybe a business deal went **WRONG**," Denny suggested.

The three sisters looked at each other in dismay, shook their heads, and sighed in unison.

"No," Tilly squeaked. "He probably just met . . ."

". . . someone from the annoying . . ." Milly continued.

". . . von Cacklefur family!" concluded Lilly.

Grumble, grumble, grunt!

EVERY RODENT FOR HIMSELF!

Shamley Rattenbaum slumped into a chair, **exhausted** from scampering home so quickly.

The triplets surrounded him, worried looks on their snouts.

"What HAPPENED, Grandpa?" Lilly asked gently.

"Are you okay?" Milly added.

But Shamley just shook his head. He was still too **breathless** to squeak.

Tilly approached with the tea tray. "Here is that **CUP** of perfectly brewed moldy tea." she offered kindly.

Shamley shook his head again and

managed to squeak out a few syllables.

"Remote control . . . *huff* . . . button . . . *puff* . . . Frankenstein . . ."

Lyrica Sonnetail's record kept playing on the gramophone, but no one seemed to be listening.

Lenny, Benny, and Denny took turns trying to squeak with Shamley.

"Where did you come from, Mr. Rattenbaum?" Lenny asked.

"If you tell us . . ." Benny continued.

". . . we might be able to figure out what you're trying to say!" finished Denny.

Shamley took a **deep** breath.

"Exhibit . . . dinos . . ." he whispered, still gasping for breath.

"Of course!" Milly cried. "He went to the dinosaur **exhibition**!"

"How was the exhibition, Grandpa?" the triplets asked in unison.

Rattenbaum didn't answer, but he looked **terrified**. He began to wave his arms frantically, pointing at the path he had taken to get home.

Ziggy noticed something coming toward them, but he just turned back to the gramophone.

The spoo... spook...

NO ONE EVER LISTENED TO HIM ANYWAY!

"The spoo ... spook ... " Shamley stammered.

Lenny interrupted him.

"Yes, we also want to see the **SPOOKOSAURUS**," he said patiently.

"It's the main attraction," Benny continued.

"They say it's absolutely **bone-chilling**!" Denny concluded.

Shamley finally had his squeak back.

"**THE SPOOKOSAURUS IS HERE!**" he shouted, pointing wildly at the path leading up to the mansion.

The other mice all turned to see the skeleton of a colossal dinosaur come bounding toward them. The beast was

moving its head and paws **BACK** and *FORTH* and snapping its claws to the beat of the music.

TAP, TAP, TAP, TAP!

It looked like the skeleton was dancing! If the spookosaurus hadn't been so terrifying, it might have been *funny* to watch. But Lenny, Benny, and Denny didn't find it amusing at all.

"**RUN FOR YOUR LIVES!**" they shouted, scurrying as fast as their paws could carry them.

"Don't leave us!" the triplets replied, terrified. But the Vandervermers had already **hightailed it** away.

Put Me Down, Bonehead!

In their haste, the three brothers **KNOCKED OVER** the little table with the tea tray, cups, and week-old pastries. Ziggy dove after the sweets and gobbled them up in one **GULP**. Unfortunately, Lenny, Benny, and Denny **BUMPED** into the unattended gramophone as well. The

ancient contraption — Shamley Rattenbaum's pride and joy from his long-ago youth — **SMASHED** into tiny pieces.

CRASH! BANG! CLUNK! BOOM!

Lyrica's record flew off the gramophone. And as soon as the music stopped, the spookosaurus went berserk. It bellowed ANGRILY, shattering the few unbroken windows that remained in the Rattenbaum Mansion.

ROAAARRRRRR!

Stop right there!

PETRIFIED with fear, the triplets were unable to move.

But Shamley Rattenbaum was suddenly filled with a protective instinct.

He leaped from his chair and *gallantly* put himself between the spookosaurus and his granddaughters like a furry shield.

"Stop right there, you **UGLY BEAST**!" he squeaked. "Don't you dare put that horrid snout of yours any closer to my *adorable* granddaughters!"

The empty-eyed spookosaurus just glared at Rattenbaum, looking more *MENACING* than ever. Slowly, it moved its bony snout closer, sniffing the aristocrat from the ends of his whiskers to the tip of his tail.

"*YUM!*" the skeleton growled clearly.

Then the spookosaurus grabbed Rattenbaum by the collar of his tattered jacket and  him off the ground.

"Put me down, Bonehead!" Shamley squeaked. "Put me down **RIGHT NOW**!"

The sisters ran to **HELP**. Tilly and Lilly

grabbed the skeleton's tail, while Milly went after one of the prehistoric monster's legs.

"Let go of our Grandpa right now!" they squeaked.

The spookosaurus nonchalantly wagged its tail, pushing Tilly and Lilly aside. Then it shook its leg, dislodging Milly. Finally, the beast tucked Rattenbaum firmly under its armpit, trapping him securely. As Shamley was jostled around, a dozen or so small bones rained down. Not one to miss an opportunity for free food, Ziggy grabbed a bone and tried to gnaw it. Unfortunately, he found it too hard and threw it away, disappointed.

Rattenbaum couldn't move a whisker.

"I told you to put me down!" he shrieked.

"And your armpit **stinks!**"

The spookosaurus just **sneered** and galloped down the path. In a few seconds, it had **disappeared** completely from sight. The triplets tried to follow, but the scampering skeleton was too **FAST**.

"Come back!" Milly, Tilly, and Lilly squeaked, but to no avail.

The sound of a car horn behind them **startled** the sisters. They turned to see the **Turborapid 3000** pull up with Creepella and Geronimo inside. As soon as

they saw the famouse publisher, they ran toward the car, begging for help.

"Help us, Geronimo! Please help!"

You're a Genius, Grandpa!

"**The monster grabbed our grandfather . . .**" moaned Tilly.

"*. . . and took him away . . .*" sobbed Milly.

"*. . . without looking back!*" whined Lilly.

Creepella sighed.

"Let's try to remain calm," she said. "We'll help you."

The rest of the von Cacklefur family had just pulled up, and they nodded in agreement.

"Where did the spookosaurus go?"

Creepella asked the triplets.

"We don't know!" they whimpered through their tears. "He was moving faster than a freight train!"

Suddenly, three heads POPPED OUT from behind the trunk of a nearby tree. It was the Vandervermer triplets!

"It was RUNNING toward the center of Gloomeria!" they declared.

"I saw it, too!" Grandpa Frankenstein agreed. He had just arrived on the scene. "That ancient fossil was holding that little fool Rattenbaum tightly under its arm!"

"Grandpa!" Creepella cried. "Did you find a solution?"

The professor chuckled.

"It wasn't easy," he admitted. "I had to look through all the books in my laboratory and in the library at Cacklefur Castle. But I finally figured it out! To stop the spookosaurus, we have to sing him the same lullaby we've been singing in our family for centuries — the **VON CACKLEFUR FAMILY LULLABY!**"

"Well, rattle my bones!" Creepella squeaked, *hugging* her grandfather. **"YOU'RE A GENIUS!"**

But Geronimo was worried.

"A lullaby?" he repeated. "But will it work forever? Won't the dinosaur just wake up again when the music stops?"

"Actually, no, dear Geronimo!" Grandfather

scoffed. "The VON CACKLEFUR FAMILY LULLABY is extremely POWERFUL. It makes monsters fall asleep . . . forever!"

Meanwhile, Shivereen noticed Ziggy staring sadly at the broken gramophone. She went over to console the poor millipede, offering him sugar-coated mosquito eggs. Ziggy devoured them in a second and perked up instantly. He licked Shivereen's face in gratitude and chirped a thank-you.

Really?

"ZIGGU! ZIP ZIG ZIG ZURP!"

Ziggu!

Shivereen smiled and went over to her aunt.

"Ziggy just told

YOU'RE A GENIUS, GRANDPA!

me something that might be helpful," she explained. "He said the spookosaurus really liked the music that was playing earlier. Ziggy said it looked like the dinosaur was dancing in perfect rhythm!"

Creepella beamed.

"Awesome!" she exclaimed. "Then we're on the right track! If the spookosaurus LIKES music, it will love the von Cacklefur family lullaby. Problem solved!"

Hmmm . . . really?

"Problem solved!" all the von Cacklefurs repeated in unison.

Geronimo was the only one who was still concerned.

"W-what's solved?" he asked, worried.

Creepella rolled her eyes.

"Geronimo, do I have to explain EVERYTHING?" she asked with a sigh. "The spookosaurus likes music, so we just have to sing him the VON CACKLEFUR FAMILY LULLABY. Then the dino will fall into a DEEP SLEEP that will last forever, and Gloomeria will be saved. Got it?"

But Geronimo wasn't convinced.

"Do you really think this lullaby will work?" he asked, still skeptical.

"Of course it will!" Boris squeaked impatiently. "The von Cacklefur family is full of great ARTISTS, and this lullaby is a true masterpiece!"

THE VON CACKLEFUR FAMILY LULLABY

Hush little dino, don't give a roar,

Here's your cozy bed in a tiny drawer.

If that drawer's too full of stinky socks,

You can always sleep in this broken box.

If that broken box has too many nails,

Here's a gloomy tomb for your dino tail.

If that gloomy tomb's too dank and musty,

The kitchen pantry's just a little crusty.

If the kitchen pantry smells of rotten oats,

You can always sleep in the chilly moat.

If the chilly moat makes you turn blue-lipped,

We'll lock you up in the castle crypt.

In the castle crypt you'll sleep forever,

Thanks to this song so sweet and clever!

THE HONOR IS YOURS, GERONIMO!

Even the Rattenbaums were impressed.

"That sounds superbly morbid!" the triplets exclaimed, clapping their paws.

"Now the only thing left to do is find the spookosaurus, jump on its back, and sing the lullaby!" exclaimed Creepella.

"**PROBLEM SOLVED!**" the von Cacklefurs cheered again.

But Geronimo had a **bad** feeling.

"Why do we have

to JUMP on the spookosaurus's back?" he asked nervously.

"Isn't it obvious?" Creepella replied. "Lullabies need to be sung softly, sweetly, and soothingly directly into an ear for them to work!"

"But w-who's going to be courageous enough to jump on that scary skeleton's back?" Geronimo asked, his whiskers twitching with fear.

"Oh, Geronimo," Creepella squeaked coyly, "I knew you'd be BRAVE enough to volunteer. The honor is all yours!"

The entire von Cacklefur family approved.

The honor is all yours!

"The honor is all yours, Geronimo!" they cried in unison.

The Rattenbaum triplets squeezed him in an enormouse hug.

Our hero!

"You're our hero!" they squeaked.

The poor journalist **fainted** on the spot. When he woke, it was to the sound of Creepella's ringtone, a **mournful** funeral march.

DUM DUM DA-DUM DUM DA-DUM DA-DUM DA-DUM!

"Hello?" she answered. It was Mayor Chatterpaws.

"Creepella, did you come up with a plan?" the mayor asked frantically. "Please hurry!

The spookosaurus is heading toward city hall!"

Creepella, it's almost here!

ROOOOOOOOAAAAAAAARRR!

Creepella heard the spookosaurus in the background and hung up on the mayor immediately.

"We have to go to city hall NOW!" she squeaked as she jumped into the Turborapid 3000. The rest of the von Cacklefurs scrambled to follow.

"Spookosaurus, we're coming for you!" they cried as they climbed into their vehicles and TOOK OFF.

A Brilliant Idea!

But Creepella didn't head straight for Gloomeria's city hall. Instead, she turned onto a **NARROW** side road: Delirium Street.

"Where are we going?" Geronimo asked, confused.

Creepella pulled up in front of a building with a **lopsided** sign hanging over the entrance.

MACABRE HISTORY MUSEUM

"I just had a brilliant idea," Creepella squeaked. She leaped out of the Turborapid 3000 and took the steps of the museum three at a time. She emerged soon after with a bright smile on her snout and four brawny, muscular rodents.

"WE'RE READY, CREEPELLA!" the most rugged of the four bellowed.

A door on the side of the museum opened to reveal a massive antique CATAPULT.

"The Museum's director gave me permission to use it," Creepella explained. "It dates back to medieval times, when King Fuzzypaw the Lion-Hearted reigned in Mysterious Valley. It's very old, but don't worry — it still works perfectly!"

King Fuzzypaw the Lion-Hearted

The four musclemice pulled the massive machine out of the museum's doors and into the street. One of them also carried a basket containing what looked like some wooden ARMOR and a HELMET made from half a coconut shell.

Geronimo looked first at the basket and then at the catapult. A cold shiver ran down his fur as a frightening new thought seized him. What was that armor for? And what was Creepella's brilliant idea?

Creepella followed Geronimo's gaze and guessed his thoughts.

"Oh, that's the armor to PR⊙+EC+ you when they hurl you onto the spookosaurus's back, Geronimo!" she squeaked.

"Mummified mummies!" Geronimo shrieked. "No way. Absolutely not! I will **not** be hurled by an ancient catapult!"

Geronimo didn't waste another second. He hightailed it out of there *immediately*! But unfortunately . . . ① Snip and Snap tripped him . . . ② He fell *ungracefully* into a stinging-nettle bush . . . ③ And Boris von Cacklefur grabbed him by the collar and dragged him out of the bush.

"Don't worry," Boris squeaked reassuringly.

"If you end up plastered to the ground like a rodent pancake, I promise to hold a whisker-lickingly gloomy **funeral** for you. I'll even compose a funeral ode for the occasion at NO EXTRA COST!"

"I'll SING the famous aria *An Extraordinary Mouse Lies Here!*" promised Madam La Tomb.

"How wonderful," Geronimo mumbled as he resigned himself to his fate. What else could he do?

Chin up, Geronimo!

③

Sigh!

Geronimo and the von Cacklefurs followed the four musclemice as they PUSHeD the catapult all the way to city hall.

As soon as they arrived, the mayor burst through the crowd. He was carrying a TROMBONE.

"What's that?" asked Shivereen.

"It's a precious family heirloom that I keep on exhibit at city hall," Mayor Chatterpaws said. "I don't want the spookosaurus to CRUSH it the way it destroyed the *Statue of the Heartbroken Knight.*"

He gestured toward the once-famous statue in the middle of the square in front of city hall.

"It's in PIECES!" he squeaked. "Not even a whisker was spared.

"It was the symbol of Gloomeria," Mayor Chatterpaws continued, wiping a tear from

his snout. "It was our *pride* and **joy** . . ."

"Let's not dwell on a marble statue," Creepella interrupted impatiently. "There's real fur on the line here! We have no time to lose — we need to launch Geronimo *immediately*!"

I'M DYING FROM THE STENCH!

The musclemice pushed the catapult into position. The spookosaurus was too busy **trampling** what was left of the statue to notice. But Shamley saw what was happening. He was still trapped under the skeleton's armpit.

"**SAVE ME!**" Shamley shouted. "**I'M DYING FROM THE STENCH!**"

Creepella put the helmet on Geronimo's head and helped him put on the armor.

"You'll be totally safe with this on," she said encouragingly. Then she led the trembling journalist to the CATAPULT.

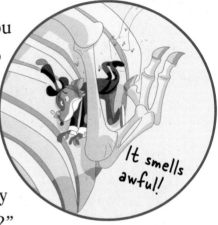

It smells awful!

"But how do you know that?" Geronimo asked nervously. "No one's ever used this catapult to fling a mouse at a dinosaur fossil before! And why does it have to be ME?"

"Stop whining, Geronimo!" Creepella scolded him. Then she turned toward the four musclemice. "Are you ready to launch the mouse?"

"We are, Creepella!" they replied *enthusiastically*. One musclemouse was holding an **enormouse** pair of scissors. He was about to cut the rope that held back the arm of the catapult.

"**Then cut it!**" Creepella cried.

The musclemouse snipped the rope and

Geronimo went flying **UP, UP, UP** into the air.

"AAAAAAAAAAHHHHHH!"

he cried.

Then he began to fall **DOWN, DOWN, DOWN** . . .

"AAAAAAAAAAHHHHHHH!"

he shrieked as he landed on the spookosaurus's back with an enormouse **THUD**!

"Yay!" the von Cacklefurs cried, applauding. "What a perfect launch!"

The spookosaurus wasn't happy at all about the new arrival. It began to wiggle from side to side, trying to shake Geronimo loose.

Geronimo clung desperately to one of the bones that protruded from the dinosaur's spine.

"**HELP!**" he squeaked. "I'm so scared!"

"Pretend you're a **cowboy** in a rodeo!" suggested Snip and Snap.

So Geronimo straddled the spookosaurus like a horse.

"Whoa! Whoa!" he kept repeating until the dinosaur finally stopped fidgeting.

Help!

"Now sing him the **LULLABY**!" shouted Boris.

Geronimo climbed up closer to the spookosaurus's ear. Then in a trembling voice he began to sing:

"Hush little dino, don't give a roar . . ."

As if by magic, the dinosaur began to **calm down**.

"It's working!" Creeepella shouted.

"**IT'S WORKING!**" the others agreed.

"It's seems to be working a little **too** well!" squeaked Shivereen. She pointed at the dino.

"What in Gloomeria . . ." began Tilly.

". . . is that dinosaur doing . . ." continued Milly.

". . . with our grandpa?" concluded Lilly.

The spookosaurus had taken Shamley out from under its arm. The giant fossil was holding and **rocking** the aristocrat gently like a newborn mouseling as Geronimo sang.

"If the chilly moat makes you turn blue-lipped . . ."

"Oh, it's so sweet!" Grandma Crypt squeaked, moved at the unexpected sight.

WE'LL LOCK YOU UP IN THE CASTLE CRYPT

Geronimo kept singing to the spookosaurus, which was almost completely asleep.

"We'll lock you up in the castle crypt . . ."

As the lullaby came to an end, Creepella shouted to Shamley.

"Come on, Shamley!" she squeaked. "Jump down!"

But it was impossible. As soon as Rattenbaum wriggled himself free, the spookosaurus grabbed him up again. It seemed the dinosaur didn't want Shamley to fall!

"Maybe we could give him something else

to cradle," Shivereen suggested.

"Yes, but what?" Creepella replied.

"There is something you could use . . ." the mayor's wife whispered softly.

"What did you say, dear?" Mayor Chatterpaws asked.

"There is something they could use, dear," Carol repeated. "Your trombone!"

We need a diversion!

"But it's a family heirloom!" the mayor protested. "It belonged to my great-great-grandfather's great-great-great-grandfather's great-great-great . . ."

"The trombone!" his wife repeated decisively.

The rest happened very QUICKLY. The mayor

Good-bye, sweetheart!

threw the trombone up to the spookosaurus, and the dinosaur grabbed it instinctively. Once Shamley was free, he jumped down to safety. The dinosaur began to gently rock the instrument as it drifted off to sleep. Meanwhile, Geronimo swiftly scampered off the spookosaurus's back.

A few seconds later the dinosaur had fallen into a deep Forever Sleep, all thanks to the VON CACKLEFUR FAMILY LULLABY. The spookosaurus was once again a giant, immobile fossil. But it wasn't inside the Gloomeria Science Museum. Instead, it was in the middle of the town square, right where the *Statue of the Heartbroken Knight* had been!

"Now how are we going to MOVE it from here?" the mayor asked with a groan.

"Why do we have to move it?" Carol asked her husband. "It looks perfectly fine where it is. And it's a lot better than that horrible statue!"

Everyone in the square agreed. Then they rushed to surround and congratulate Geronimo.

"YOU'RE OUR HERO!" the triplets squeaked as they hugged him tightly. Then they turned to Creepella and thanked her, too.

But Shamley was still too ANGRY with his longtime nemesis, Grandpa Frankenstein. He couldn't bring himself to thank any of the von Cacklefurs for saving him. Instead he stormed home, grumbling to himself the entire way.

Benny, Denny, and Lenny Vandervermer approached the triplets.

"Now that your grandfather is okay, why don't we go back to our little party?" they suggested. Then each brother took one of the triplets' arms.

Let's go, my dears!

The mayor jumped at the word.

"Did I hear the word **PARTY**?" he asked. "We absolutely must throw an unforgettable bash to celebrate our hero, Geronimo!"

"Actually," Geronimo protested timidly, "if you don't mind, I'd rather go back to writing my ENCYCLOPEDIA OF GHOSTS."

But Creepella wouldn't hear of it.

"Forget it!" she squeaked. "Even though you were a complete 'fraidy mouse, the

mayor is right. You were a real hero today, Geronimo, and we have to celebrate!"

The mayor presented Geronimo with an enormouse **rusted** key.

"In the name of all of Gloomeria, I give you this key to the city," he declared. "Because in these dark times . . ."

His wife tugged at his jacket, and the mayor immediately stopped the speech he had begun.

"I mean, let's celebrate!" he cried.

Everyone cheered.

"HOORAY FOR GERONIMO!"

"Hooray for the von Cacklefur Family!"

"Hooray for Mysterious Valley!"

YOU'RE SO BRAVE, UNCLE G.!

A shiver ran down my fur as I finished reading the book. I had almost forgotten how **scared** I had been during that *incredible* adventure.

My nephew Benjamin's eyes were filled with admiration.

"What a book!" he exclaimed. "It's the most whisker-chewing, tail-paralyzing story I've ever heard! And you were so **BRAVE**, Uncle G. —"

"I was scared stiff," I admitted to my nephew. "But when there was no other choice, I guess I found the courage!"

"I hope someone destroyed Grandfather Frankenstein's horrible invention." Benjamin shuddered.

"Oh, yes. It will never be used again."

"Will you publish Creepella's new book?" Benjamin asked.

"Of course!" I replied. "In fact, I'll **text** her right now to let her know."

She replied a few seconds later with her own text:

I'm so happy, Geronimo! I'll let everyone in Gloomeria know. We can have a book signing party and Chef Stewrat will prepare his special spookosaurus stew for everyone!

My stomach lurched just thinking about Chef Stewrat's awful cooking. But thinking of food made me realize I was hungry. I put down my cell phone and asked Benjamin if he wanted to go for an ice cream. He happily agreed.

"Let's go to Tutti Frutti," he said. "I'll bet Lickety Splitz has invented a NEW flavor since the last time I was there!"

When we arrived at the ice-cream shop,

Lickety suggested I try the new flavor.

It was LIZARD GREEN and covered with small white sprinkles.

"What is it?" I asked, intrigued.

"Herbed-cheese ice cream topped with goat cheese sprinkles," he replied proudly. "I call it **Dinosaur Scales**! So, what do you say? Want to try it?"

Dinosaur Scales!

What a strange flavor!

What is it?

"Um, no, thank you!" I replied. I was done with **DINOSAURS** for a while. But I would be sure to bring a pint to Creepella and the von Cacklefurs on my next visit to Gloomeria. I was sure they would appreciate such an *unusual* flavor. After all, they were a very *unusual* family!

But being unique made the von Cacklefurs special. And Creepella truly was the *best* writer in Mysterious Valley. I knew her latest book was going to be a spooktacular **BESTSELLER**!

See you on my next adventure!

If you liked this book, be sure to check out my other adventures!

#1 THE THIRTEEN GHOSTS

#2 MEET ME IN HORRORWOOD

#3 GHOST PIRATE TREASURE

#4 RETURN OF THE VAMPIRE

#5 FRIGHT NIGHT

#6 RIDE FOR YOUR LIFE!

#7 A SUITCASE FULL OF GHOSTS

#8 THE PHANTOM OF THE THEATER

#9 THE HAUNTED DINOSAUR

Be sure to read all my fabumouse adventures!

#1 Lost Treasure of the Emerald Eye

#2 The Curse of the Cheese Pyramid

#3 Cat and Mouse in a Haunted House

#4 I'm Too Fond of My Fur!

#5 Four Mice Deep in the Jungle

#6 Paws Off, Cheddarface!

#7 Red Pizzas for a Blue Count

#8 Attack of the Bandit Cats

#9 A Fabumouse Vacation for Geronimo

#10 All Because of a Cup of Coffee

#11 It's Halloween, You 'Fraidy Mouse!

#12 Merry Christmas, Geronimo!

#13 The Phantom of the Subway

#14 The Temple of the Ruby of Fire

#15 The Mona Mousa Code

#16 A Cheese-Colored Camper

#17 Watch Your Whiskers, Stilton!

#18 Shipwreck on the Pirate Islands

#19 My Name Is Stilton, Geronimo Stilton

#20 Surf's Up, Geronimo!

#21 The Wild, Wild West

#22 The Secret of Cacklefur Castle

A Christmas Tale

#23 Valentine's Day Disaster

#24 Field Trip to Niagara Falls

#25 The Search for Sunken Treasure

#26 The Mummy with No Name

#27 The Christmas Toy Factory

#28 Wedding Crasher

#29 Down and Out Down Under

#30 The Mouse Island Marathon

#31 The Mysterious Cheese Thief

Christmas Catastrophe

#32 Valley of the Giant Skeletons

#33 Geronimo and the Gold Medal Mystery

#34 Geronimo Stilton, Secret Agent

#35 A Very Merry Christmas

#36 Geronimo's Valentine

#37 The Race Across America

#38 A Fabumouse School Adventure

#39 Singing Sensation

#40 The Karate Mouse

#41 Mighty Mount Kilimanjaro

#42 The Peculiar Pumpkin Thief

#43 I'm Not a Supermouse!

#44 The Giant Diamond Robbery

#45 Save the White Whale!

#46 The Haunted Castle

#47 Run for the Hills, Geronimo!

#48 The Mystery in Venice

#49 The Way of the Samurai

#50 This Hotel Is Haunted!

#51 The Enormouse Pearl Heist

#52 Mouse in Space!

#53 Rumble in the Jungle

#54 Get into Gear, Stilton!

#55 The Golden Statue Plot

#56 Flight of the Red Bandit

The Hunt for the Golden Book

#57 The Stinky Cheese Vacation

#58 The Super Chef Contest

#59 Welcome to Moldy Manor

The Hunt for the Curious Cheese

#60 The Treasure of Easter Island

#61 Mouse House Hunter

#62 Mouse Overboard!

The Hunt for the Secret Papyrus

#63 The Cheese Experiment

#64 Magical Mission

#65 Bollywood Burglary

The Hunt for the Hundredth Key

#66 Operation: Secret Recipe

#67 The Chocolate Chase

Don't miss any of my adventures in the Kingdom of Fantasy!

THE KINGDOM OF FANTASY

THE QUEST FOR PARADISE:
THE RETURN TO THE KINGDOM OF FANTASY

THE AMAZING VOYAGE:
THE THIRD ADVENTURE IN THE KINGDOM OF FANTASY

THE DRAGON PROPHECY:
THE FOURTH ADVENTURE IN THE KINGDOM OF FANTASY

THE VOLCANO OF FIRE:
THE FIFTH ADVENTURE IN THE KINGDOM OF FANTASY

THE SEARCH FOR TREASURE:
THE SIXTH ADVENTURE IN THE KINGDOM OF FANTASY

THE ENCHANTED CHARMS:
THE SEVENTH ADVENTURE IN THE KINGDOM OF FANTASY

THE PHOENIX OF DESTINY:
AN EPIC KINGDOM OF FANTASY ADVENTURE

THE HOUR OF MAGIC:
THE EIGHTH ADVENTURE IN THE KINGDOM OF FANTASY

THE WIZARD'S WAND:
THE NINTH ADVENTURE IN THE KINGDOM OF FANTASY

THE SHIP OF SECRETS:
THE TENTH ADVENTURE IN THE KINGDOM OF FANTASY

THE DRAGON OF FORTUNE:
AN EPIC KINGDOM OF FANTASY ADVENTURE

Don't miss any of these exciting Thea Sisters adventures!

Thea Stilton and the Dragon's Code

Thea Stilton and the Mountain of Fire

Thea Stilton and the Ghost of the Shipwreck

Thea Stilton and the Secret City

Thea Stilton and the Mystery in Paris

Thea Stilton and the Cherry Blossom Adventure

Thea Stilton and the Star Castaways

Thea Stilton: Big Trouble in the Big Apple

Thea Stilton and the Ice Treasure

Thea Stilton and the Secret of the Old Castle

Thea Stilton and the Blue Scarab Hunt

Thea Stilton and the Prince's Emerald

Thea Stilton and the Mystery on the Orient Express

Thea Stilton and the Dancing Shadows

Thea Stilton and the Legend of the Fire Flowers

Thea Stilton and the Spanish Dance Mission

Thea Stilton and the Journey to the Lion's Den

**Thea Stilton and the
Great Tulip Heist**

**Thea Stilton and the
Chocolate Sabotage**

Thea Stilton and the
Missing Myth

Thea Stilton and the
Lost Letters

**Thea Stilton and the
Tropical Treasure**

Thea Stilton and the
Hollywood Hoax

Thea Stilton and the
Madagascar Madness

Thea Stilton and the
Frozen Fiasco

Up Next!

**Thea Stilton and the
Venice Masquerade**

And check out my fabumouse special editions!

THEA STILTON:
THE JOURNEY
TO ATLANTIS

THEA STILTON:
THE SECRET OF
THE FAIRIES

THEA STILTON:
THE SECRET OF
THE SNOW

THEA STILTON:
THE CLOUD
CASTLE

THEA STILTON:
THE TREASURE
OF THE SEA

THEA STILTON:
THE LAND OF
FLOWERS

1. Mountains of the Mangy Yeti
2. Cacklefur Castle
3. Angry Walnut Tree
4. Rattenbaum Mansion
5. Rancidrat River
6. Bridge of Shaky Steps
7. Squeakspeare Mansion
8. Slimy Swamp
9. Ogre Highway
10. Gloomeria
11. Shivery Arts Academy
12. Horrorwood Studios

1. Oozing moat

2. Drawbridge

3. Grand entrance

4. Moldy basement

5. Patio, with a view of the moat

6. Dusty library

7. Room for unwanted guests

8. Mummy room

9. Watchtower

10. Creaking staircase

11. Banquet room

12. Garage (for antique hearses)

13. Bewitched tower

14. Garden of carnivorous plants

15. Stinky kitchen

16. Crocodile pool and piranha tank

17. Creepella's room

18. Tower of musky tarantulas

19. Bitewing's tower (with antique contraptions)

DEAR MOUSE FRIENDS,
GOOD-BYE UNTIL
THE NEXT BOOK!